I'm a Spinosaurus
Bigger Than a T-Rex

Written by
Carter Pendergast &
Katherine Pendergast

I am a dinosaur all creatures should fear.

I growl, grunt, and hunt. All scatter when I'm near.

They call me Spinosaurus.

I'm the largest land carnivore because I am enormous.

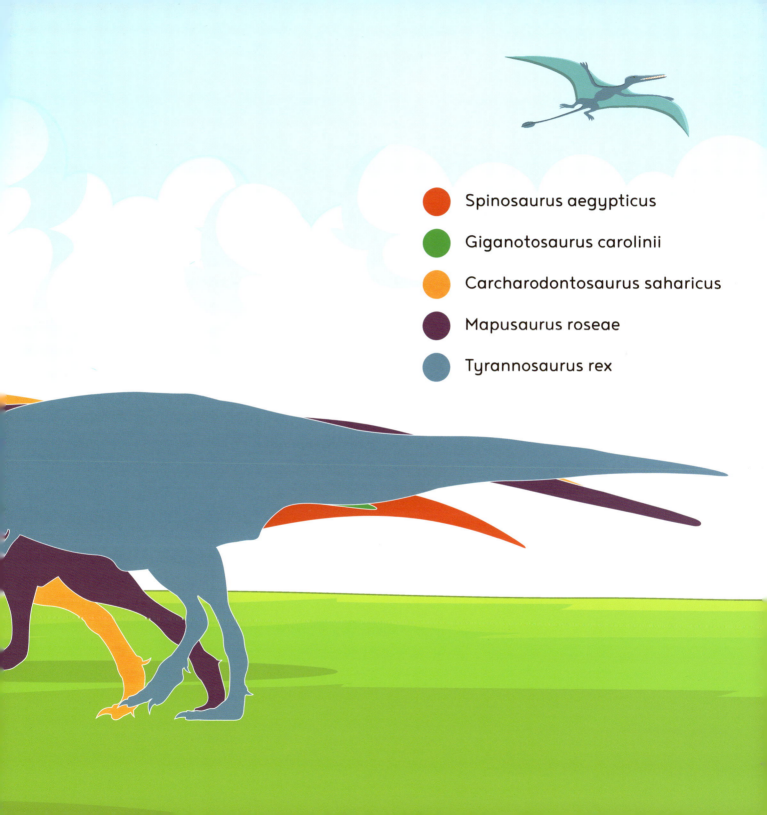

From the base of my neck to the start of my tail, you will find a giant sail.

Did it help me catch fish, cool down, or scare foes?

When I went out for a hike, I scared land and sea creatures alike.

My paddle-like tail and powerful limbs make me a dinosaur that could swim!

There is no doubt,
I have a long, crocodile snout.
My favorite dish
is a mighty big fish.

On two legs I can stand tall,
or I can sink down and crawl.

I am hard to hide
with my unusual stride.

People want to know more about me.
I'm a bit of a mystery and a big part of history.
My bones are quite rare.
So, please handle with care.

Fun Facts about a Spinosaurus

For many years, scientists believed that a T-Rex was the largest land carnivore, but today the largest known land carnivore is a Spinosaurus.

Experts believe the Spinosaurus's large spine supported its sail.

The sail was gigantic, measuring up to 7 feet (2.1 m) tall.

Spinosaurus

Height: 20 ft (6 m)
Length: 52.5 ft (16 m)
Weight: 9.9 tons (9 tonnes)

Experts believe Spinosaurus spent time on land and in the water. Features such as long and strong arms, a long flexible tail, nostrils near the top of the snout, dense bones, and webbed feet indicate that Spinosaurus could swim underwater.

Experts believe the Spinosaurus's crocodilian snout and needle-like teeth were perfect for piercing slippery fish.

A Spinosaurus skull was around 6 feet (1.8 m) long.

Only a few mostly complete fossilized skeletons have been discovered. In 1944, a World War II bombing raid destroyed one of the precious few.

Experts believe Spinosaurus mostly walked on two legs (known as biped), but they could also walk on all four legs (known as quadruped).

What is your favorite dinosaur?

Work Cited:

Hibbert, Clare. *Children's Encyclopedia of Dinosaurs*. London: Arcturus Publishing Limited, 2020.

Woodward, John. *The Dinosaur Book* (Smithsonian). New York: DK Publishing, 2018.

Carter Pendergast Photo Credit: Lyra Lee Photography.

Published by Kat's Socks

Bismarck, ND USA

www.katssocks.com

Text, illustration, and design copyright © 2021 Kat's Socks

All rights reserved. No part of this publication may be reproduced in whole or in part, or stored in a retrieval system, or transmitted in any form or by any means, electronic, mechanical, photocopying, recording, or otherwise, without written permission of the publisher.

ISBN 978-1-7351053-3-8

Library of Congress Control Number: 2020924508

Printed in China

Carter Pendergast

Carter is an energetic six-year-old who loves dinosaurs and dreams of becoming a paleontologist someday, so he can continue his love of studying dinosaurs. His favorite dinosaur is the Spinosaurus. He loves sharing fun facts about this massive dinosaur with everyone he meets. Carter lives in Bismarck, North Dakota, with his family and two dogs.

Katherine Pendergast

Katherine loves reading to her son, Carter, about dinosaurs. He wanted to write about his favorite dinosaur, the Spinosaurus, and together they made *I'm a Spinosaurus, Bigger Than a T-Rex* a reality. Katherine lives in Bismarck, North Dakota, with her family and two dogs. She is also the author of *Pickles the Dog, Adopted*; *Pickles the Dog, A Christmas Tradition*; *Pickles the Dog, Goes to School*; *Babies of the Badlands*; and coauthor of *In Loving Memory, A Child's Journey to Understanding a Funeral and Starting the Grieving Process* and *In Loving Memory, A Child's Journey to Understanding a Cremation Funeral and Starting the Grieving Process*.